The Beginning

Book 5

My New Normal

Sara Michelle

SADDLEBACK
EDUCATIONAL PUBLISHING

The Aftermath * Book 1
The Inside * Book 2
The Others * Book 3
The Outside * Book 4
The Beginning * Book 5

SADDLEBACK
EDUCATIONAL PUBLISHING
www.sdlback.com

ISBN-13: 978-1-61651-785-4
ISBN-10: 1-61651-785-9
eBook: 978-1-61247-354-3

Printed in Guangzhou, China
0812/CA21201148

16 15 14 13 12   1 2 3 4 5

Day 18

5:30 p.m.

It took me a few seconds after seeing Jason in the headlight to comprehend that it was *the* Jason standing there. I then realized that Jesska had absolutely no idea who Jason was or the potential danger we were in. Forget potential. We were in danger. Jason had promised that he would be back, and unfortunately, it looked like he kept his promises. Just my luck.

"Who the hell?" Jesska asked, glancing at me nervously. The headlight was the only source of light available in the warehouse, and I was determined to keep it shining bright.

"Jesska," I whispered. "I need you to stay in the car. And whatever you do, don't let the headlight go dark. Okay?"

I looked into her eyes and saw confusion, fear, and just a little sass. I knew she would have my back.

"Who *is* Jason? You *know* him?" she muttered frantically.

I nodded. "He was with us in the shelter. We kicked him out because he was a threat. Dangerous. Possibly crazy. It's a long story."

I slowly climbed through the passenger side window out onto the concrete floor. I walked forward, pulling my shoulders back, trying to make myself look as built as possible.

The headlight gave Jason an eerie glow. He looked like a specter. Truly creepy. My heart raced as I realized how unprepared I was for this confrontation. If this was war, my chances were slim to none. We both stared at each other before a slow smirk spread across his face.

"Rrry-aan!" he boomed.

His large pupils seemed dilated in the light, and his speech was slurred. For sure he was high. I crossed my arms over my chest.

Jason moved forward slowly, menacingly, and kept the creepy smirk on his face. His act was almost theatrical.

"I knew we'd be meeting again," he stated, wobbling slightly. He was definitely messed up on something. Could be beneficial, I thought. But also totally dangerous.

I cleared my throat and deepened my voice. "So you say," I replied.

I heard Jesska snort behind me. Ha-ha! Only she would make fun of me during a life or death situation. I decided to lose the deep voice.

"What do you want, Jason?" I asked.

"I don't want anything, kid," Jason replied firmly, standing straighter. "But you piss me off. And I don't like it when people piss me off."

Great, just great. I had a trashed a-hole ready to kill me and no 9-1-1 to call. I was completely alone.

I dropped my shoulders, knowing that nothing I pretended to do would stop this man from hurting me if he really wanted to.

"Who's your friend?" Jason asked, leering at Jesska. He raised his eyes and turned to wink at her. He actually winked at her.

"What the—" Jesska stated.

I lunged toward Jason and shoved him with as much force as I could. The fact that I was angry helped, and Jason grunted, surprised, and fell back. He landed with a thud and angrily turned his head up toward me.

"You just made a big mistake, kid."

He shook his fist at me as he struggled to get himself upright. The fact that he was messed up slowed him down, and I hoped that it would be enough for me to do what I had to do.

"Let's get him, Ryan," Jesska said firmly, suddenly by my side. I shook my head. I couldn't let her get involved in this. She could easily be killed.

"Get back in the truck, Jesska," I ordered.

She laughed. "There's nothing you can do to make me get back in the Hummer. Deal with it." She walked ahead of me over toward Jason, and I knew she was completely right. That girl would not be ordered around.

Jason was standing now, and he looked challengingly at Jesska, who had her arms crossed less than two feet away from him.

"Look, slobbers," she said calmly. Jason slowly wiped a small line of drool that had begun dripping down his chin. Gross.

"We can do this the easy way, or we can do this the hard way," she stated flatly.

I couldn't believe the kind of nerve that Jesska had. I watched from farther back, feeling like a wuss.

Jason laughed. His laugh was loud and thick. He reminded me of one of those filthy cowboys you would see in old western films. I had no idea what was about to happen next. My heart raced, and the silence in the room was thick, almost muggy. Jason breathed heavily, and Jesska glared at him.

He seemed thrown off by the idea that Jesska was the one who was confronting him. I wondered if he was still willing to do anything to get his hands on me.

Jason and Jesska were now standing eye to eye. Jesska held her ground firmly and clenched her fists as she stared Jason down. Jason tried his best to maintain a challenging look in his eyes, but every so often they would roll back slightly or his eyelids would begin to close. Whatever he had taken was affecting him more. I just hoped it was enough to give us the advantage.

Day 18

10:30 p.m.

No way was I going to let Jason win. I had people depending on me. What happened earlier needed to happen, but the brutal and bloody assault will forever be packed away in the back of my mind. As Jesska confronted Jason, he cleared his throat and shook his finger at her. "You have more balls than him." He smirked.

Jesska rolled her eyes.

Jason's smirk disappeared and was replaced with a scowl. He stepped closer to Jesska, and they were now nearly nose to nose.

I knew that it was time for me to take action. Jesska was creating a big enough diversion for me to be able to take Jason by surprise and get rid of him for good. My eyes scanned the dimly lit area, and I browsed for any sort of object that would help me to do that. They landed on a thick metal rod that looked like a leg from a large tripod. I decided that it would work as a weapon, so I then determined a way to creep over to the corner and grab it before Jason realized what I was trying to do.

I slowly moved toward my secret weapon. Jason now had his hands on

Jesska's shoulders, and I knew our time was limited.

I wrapped my fingers around the cool rod and prayed my hands wouldn't be too wet from nerves to handle it properly. My heart pounded and my knees shook. Jesska glanced anxiously toward me, and I knew that she was getting scared.

"A girl like you isn't going to survive in these conditions anyway!" Jason spat, tightening his grip on Jesska's arms.

That was it. I barely knew Jesska. If I was a heartless bastard, I would be able to dip out of this situation easily enough. I could leave Jesska and go back to the shelter with Cecilia—and everyone else—and everything would be safe and okay again. But watching him place his hands on her, I knew what I had to do.

Amazingly, my heart rate began to slow. The clamminess that I had been experiencing disappeared and was replaced with an angry, focused heat.

The way that Jason and Jesska were now positioned was perfect for my plan of attack. Jason was turned slightly away from me, exposing most of his back. Jesska was facing toward me, and although it was hard to see her over Jason's big head, I could tell that she was growing more and more anxious.

When she saw what I held in my hand—I nodded once, assuring her that I would go through with it—her eyes glistened.

I crept over behind Jason and held up the rod to swing. Just as I did, Jason lunged and shoved Jesska hard, slamming her into a wall. Before I knew what I was doing, I swung, smashing the metal rod into the side of Jason's head.

Jason wailed in agony as a pool of blood began streaming from the right side of his temple. My stomach roiled. Blood had always made me nauseous. I swallowed hard and quickly made my way over to Jesska, who was lying still.

I ignored Jason's groans, realizing that Jesska could be seriously injured.

I leaned over her and winced. A large bruise was forming on the left side of her face. Her eyelids fluttered, but she remained quiet.

"Jesska?" I whispered, brushing hair out of her eyes. "Please tell me you're going to be all right," I muttered, realizing how much the idea of losing her bothered me.

She slowly opened her eyes and managed to grimace.

"Of course I'm going to be all right. Just a minor concussion, I'm sure. Did you get him?"

I glanced over at Jason, and my stomach flipped as I saw that the pool of blood around him had expanded.

"He could still be alive," I muttered. "But for the moment, he's not going anywhere."

I turned and tenderly swept my fingers across Jesska's bruised cheek. She closed her eyes and smiled.

"This is nice," she whispered softly. My stomach flipped again. But this time it wasn't because I felt like barfing. It was because Jesska's face seemed so peaceful and innocent. There was a slight smile at the corner of her plump lips. There were a few freckles that dotted her nose and upper cheekbones that I had never been close enough to notice before.

I stayed quiet. There was nothing I could do. As much as I wanted to lean over and kiss her and make her feel better, the images of Cecilia in my head made my heart ache. I looked down and saw Jesska as a normal girl for the first time. As she rested, her tough exterior disintegrated and was replaced with the vulnerability that every girl had. My head throbbed, and I debated things that I'd never had to debate before. My old life was over. I was in survival mode, and I had possibly just killed someone. But the only thing I could think of was, man, am I in trouble!

Day 19

10:00 a.m.

Jesska's eyes fluttered open, and she squinted at me, examining my expression and searching my thoughts.

"Ryan," she muttered.

I mumbled something unintelligent. She sighed.

"We should probably get moving." She sat up and slowly pushed me away from her. I didn't argue. The awkwardness in the room was thick after realizing that we had slept in each other's arms. I checked out her bruised face and applied more of the ointment I'd found last night when she'd passed out. She winced a little.

I got up and walked over to where Jason lay in a bloody pool and swallowed, telling myself not to puke. I had done some pretty crazy damage to his head. The reality that I had actually killed someone began to sink in, and I suddenly felt sick to my stomach.

I felt a hand touch me lightly on the shoulder.

"It was the only thing we could do, Ryan," Jesska said soothingly. "He wasn't a good guy. He was going to kill you and do worse to me."

In the back of my head, I knew she was right. But I also knew that if

Cecilia had been the one observing, she'd have a very different outlook.

I turned toward Jesska and groaned, placing my hands on my temples.

"What do we do with the body, Jesska?" I cried, feeling on the brink of a massive freak out. Jesska suggested that we burn it since digging a grave in the frozen earth was not an option. Technically, I guess we could say he was cremated. Although it wasn't exactly what I had in mind, it would be enough to rest my anxious thoughts.

We decided to drag him on a tarp to a large pile of brush that we'd seen behind the warehouse. After a little bit of searching, I was able to come up with a large bottle of lighter fluid and some matches.

Maneuvering Jason on the tarp and dragging him a few hundred yards across a parking lot was a forty-five-minute struggle. But we didn't want to unload the Hummer—or deal with a bloody mess inside the truck—and there was little gas to spare.

The whole idea of what we were doing gave me the heebie-jeebies. My conversation with Jesska had been limited since our awkward encounter in the warehouse. I wish I could sit her down and tell her how hard it was to not give in to the mixed feelings I had for her. Eventually, I would have to. But at this point in time, I didn't have the nerve.

Watching Jason's body burning in a pile of brush gave me an odd sense of calm. The smell of smoke and lighter fluid and something else unearthly surrounded us, and when I closed my eyes to the blowing wind, it almost felt like home. The wind reminded me of all the Christmas nights I had spent with my mom on our front porch swing, sitting under Grammy's old quilt and debating whether or not the wind would knock Santa off course.

"Ryan," Jesska said, looking past the brush.

"Mmm?" I answered, looking down at the muddy, melting snow beneath my feet.

"Kiss me."

I looked up abruptly and felt my cheeks grow warm. Had I heard her right?

My eyes met hers, and at once I knew that I had not been mistaken. Her eyes had suddenly become eager. She took a step toward me, and before I could realize what was happening, her body was against mine, and all of the longing and desire that we had set aside for the past few days was released.

After a few moments, she drew back and took a deep breath. I looked into her eyes once more, expecting the same eagerness, but instead, I found them filled with something I least expected. Sadness.

She took a step back and cleared her throat.

"I honestly have no idea why the hell I just did that," she stated bluntly.

I shivered. I wondered whether to be insulted by her statement or not. I also wondered why I didn't regret kissing her. It made me feel guilty, but not as guilty as I thought I should feel. It didn't even weird me out. I loved Cecilia. I knew that for a fact. But I also knew that there was something about Jesska that I couldn't resist. I wondered why I was still experiencing high school drama in the middle of the freaking apocalypse.

A large gust of wind blew, causing both Jesska and me to look up at the sky. It was growing darker by the minute, and I knew that another storm was on its way.

Day 20

9:00 a.m.

After four days of them being gone, I wondered if Michael, Henry, and Ryan had grown to be friends—or not. This was one of those times where I really wished we still had cell service.

Renee and I decided to start taking Daniel and Brittany outside to get some exercise each day. We both agreed that it was an awful thing for young kids to see such horrible destruction, but we also agreed that this was our reality—their reality—now. Eventually, we would all have to leave the shelter, and we may as well have Brittany and Daniel start getting used to what they would have to face.

After taking the kids outside, I planned on a quick shower. Then help Renee set up for lunch. Then possibly try to take a short nap. With Ryan gone, sleep was almost impossible to accomplish, and when I did, it was brief. My plans were interrupted by Renee's worried voice.

"Cecilia," she called anxiously. I wondered what had happened this time. Renee tended to be the overly dramatic type. When we'd first met her, Ryan and I had found her obnoxious, but now, we saw her as the mom of the shelter.

I walked out of my bedroom and down the hallway, expecting to find Renee in the kitchen. Surprisingly, it was empty.

"Renee?" I called out.

"Up here, sweetie. We're ... come up here," Renee replied, her voice sounding farther away. They were on the main level of the shelter, meaning that something must have happened outside.

I walked up the long staircase, and the first thing I noticed was the temperature difference from inside the shelter. I shivered. Memories of the freezing, dark nights shortly after the earthquake played through my head, and I was suddenly overcome with dizziness.

After it passed, I slowly walked up the rest of the stairs to find Renee and Dr. Jenkins standing near the entrance to the shelter. As I approached them and looked outside, I gasped.

Thick, dark clouds had begun to roll in, covering the city. Intense gusts of wind blew every so often, shaking the remaining portion of the structure's main floor.

My heart sank as I realized that Ryan, Michael, and Henry were stuck outside in the approaching storm.

"What does it mean?" I asked, worried about the storm, which appeared more powerful than anything I'd ever seen before.

Renee and I anxiously looked at Dr. Jenkins, who was staring blankly out over the boiling horizon. A few moments passed and he sighed, turning his head toward us.

"It could mean anything," he said, shrugging his shoulders. He shook his head. "Everything our group has ever predicted is happening way too soon."

I began to lose hope, realizing the impact of that statement. There wasn't anybody in the world who really knew when or how the world was going to end. No mathematician or physicist was capable of determining something like that. Something that was completely out of our hands.

"Renee!"

"Dr. Jenkins!"

I turned. Coming from the east side of the shelter, Henry and Michael walked toward us, struggling against the wind. They had managed to scavenge backpacks and duffle bags from who knows where. I presumed that each bag was full with whatever supplies they had collected over the past few days.

I waited, scanning behind them, looking for Ryan's face. My blood turned cold when I noticed that he was nowhere to be seen.

"Ryan ..." Renee whispered.

I stood still as Henry and Michael approached us. They were breathing heavily, and their cheeks were a bright rosy-pink.

Dr. Jenkins and Renee immediately took a couple of the bags from them and ushered them into the shelter. I couldn't move. I heard hushed whispers coming from behind me, and I wondered what kind of story Michael and Henry had to tell. I wondered if I even wanted to know. A few moments later, I felt Renee's hands on my shoulders.

"Cecilia, come inside. Let's talk."

I allowed her to lead me back down into the shelter and sit me down on the couch in the main living area. The large TV still remained untouched, but the crack that had been there when we had first arrived had expanded. Renee sat across from me and crossed her ankles.

"They split up," she started. I looked up at her and raised my eyebrows, waiting for further explanation.

"He didn't want to search people's houses for supplies like Michael and Henry were doing," she explained. "Michael said that Ryan felt that it wasn't right to go through other people's things. Even if it meant surviving."

I smiled. That's something only Ryan would do.

She continued, "They were all supposed to meet back up."

My heart dropped as I realized what had happened. Ryan never showed up. My mind raced with the thousands of things that could be going wrong for him. The coat he had been wearing when he left was not heavy enough to keep him warm in this weather. I wondered if he was lost and scared.

Or worse. I gulped and tried to calm down.

I stared blankly at Renee, realizing that I had absolutely no words to say to her.

I stood up slowly and walked past everyone, not acknowledging Renee or the others as I left the room.

Day 20

10:00 a.m.

The next morning I woke up early, before Ryan, and decided to get an early start to the day. After sending Jason's body to the ever after, we had spent yesterday searching the warehouse and watching the storms come and go as the weather warmed. I knew that I needed to collect a few more things before we started back, so I spent the majority of the morning separating the things that I felt would be needed in the upcoming weeks.

After a couple of hours, I had come up with a good collection of preserved foods and clothes. I got a wide variety of sizes in everything that was warm and functional. You couldn't say that the clothes were fashionable, but at least I was trying to be thoughtful about the other people who stayed with Ryan at the shelter—even his girlfriend.

"Why didn't you wake me up?"

I jumped. I turned around and saw Ryan standing sleepily before me. Half of his long hair was sticking up, and his cheeks were bright pink.

"You looked far too peaceful to be touched," I commented and returned to packing boxes. He chuckled.

"So are we going back into town today?" he asked quietly.

I stopped packing and turned to face him. "Ready to get rid of me that quickly, huh?" I asked jokingly.

He blushed. "Not at all. Actually, I was going to ask you if you had thought any more about coming to stay at the shelter with us. I just don't like the thought of you out *there* on your own."

I remained quiet. Going back to the shelter would mean meeting *her*, the girlfriend. Going back to the shelter would mean having to watch Ryan be with the one he was really in love with—fussy, wimpy Cecilia. Oh, he told me about her. I was not going to put myself through that. No way.

I shook my head and stood up to face Ryan.

"I don't think I'm going to do that, Ryan."

He scrunched his eyebrows and almost looked disappointed.

"But why?" he asked, scratching the back of his head. "I don't see how you think you can live on your own, Jesska."

I scoffed. He obviously didn't really know me then.

I felt his hand on my shoulder and shivered. I turned toward him and narrowed my eyes.

"Ryan, the thought of moving into a shelter where you are already happily stationed with your girlfriend and friends doesn't sound too inviting to me, honestly."

Hurt flashed across his face, and I hated myself for being such a bitch all of the time.

"Jesska, I'm sorry," he said sincerely, putting both of his hands on my shoulders. I looked away and prepared for the sappy speech that I knew was going to come next. "I'm sorry that I kissed you back," he said bluntly.

I turned around, surprised by his honesty, and waited to hear what he had to say next.

"It's not that I didn't want to, Jess; honestly, I did." I smiled at my newly given nickname.

"Something about you drives me crazy," he exclaimed, turning my chin toward him. His eyes were sincere, and I knew that he was having a hard time doing this. He kept his eyes on mine and continued, "You're beautiful. You're a great girl. One of the bravest I know. We have something. It scares the hell out of me. So it's safe to say that I definitely dig you."

His eyes shined, and I wished that it were possible to lean in and kiss him again. But I knew where this was going, and I knew that in the end, I wasn't going to be the one to get him, and that's just the way it was going to have to be.

"But I love Cecilia," he stated. And in his eyes, I knew that he meant that. And his realness and honesty were so sincere that there was nothing I could do but respect him. I nodded my head.

"I know you do," I replied.

We looked at each other, and Ryan slowly leaned in and kissed me on the forehead.

It was decided that I would return to the shelter with Ryan to help him unpack the Hummer and to check the place out. I realized that I was going to be manipulated into staying with them in some way or another, but the idea of a hot shower was beginning to sound too tempting to decline. I figured if being at the shelter with them was too unbearable, then I could just take my things and leave after the weather settled down—if it did at all.

Ryan began to seem anxious to get back to the shelter. Knowing he probably missed Cecilia, I packed all of my supplies quickly and was able to have everything in its place within about an hour. Ryan had collected much more stuff than I had. In one box he had various sweaters and clothing, ranging in size and age group. Two other boxes were filled to the top with different types of food: dried fruit, canned beans, creamed corn, soup, gummy snacks, tuna, and Spam were a few of the things that we had been able to scrounge out of all the food that had spoiled. In the last large box he had collected a number of different miscellaneous items, such as batteries, flashlights, matches, some over-the-counter drugs and first aid supplies, as well as a few coloring books and a stuffed teddy bear.

"I'm pretty sure this will take up the rest of the open space in the Hummer right now," Ryan noted, looking at our stacks of boxes.

I nodded as thunder rumbled in the distance.

"What do you think is going to happen with the weather?" I asked. I was starting to get so tired of never knowing what was going to happen next. Although I was never the type of person to sit down and watch any of the news channels, I'd now be willing to give anything to see the familiar anchors on my TV screen and hear a solution to this worldwide mess. But of course, that wasn't going to be the case.

Ryan shrugged his shoulders. "Who's to say at this point? I think we've all established that right now, whatever happens next is completely unknown."

He paused and looked at me carefully. "Which is why I really—"

I groaned, knowing what was coming next. He had been pestering me about staying at the shelter all morning.

"Look, Ryan," I said firmly. "I will make the decision whether or not I want to stay at your little refugee camp once I get there and check it out." I pointed toward the boxes. "Let's load these babies up and hit the road before the next storm causes any trouble."

Day 20

12:45 p.m.

After spending several hours in my room, I determined that playing the distressed, whimpering girlfriend was not for me and certainly was not going to help Ryan. I rationalized. Ryan was smart. It wasn't like him to get lost. He would be clever enough to track his path so that he could find his way back. In my heart, I knew Ryan was not lost. Which left only two other options.

One, something had gone terribly wrong, and there was something keeping him from being able to meet Henry and Michael. Or two, he purposely had not met back up with them. I didn't really know why Ryan would just not show up, but I did know that it was something he would do if he had a good enough reason to. I wondered how long Michael and Henry had even waited for him.

After awhile, I heard a knock on my door. "Come in," I replied.

I expected to see Renee come in and start mothering me. But instead, I was surprised to find Brittany sheepishly opening the door and peeking in.

"Hey, Cecilia," she said quietly. "Can I come in for a minute?"

I turned while sitting on the bed and forced a smile on my face. "Of course."

Brittany walked in and stood a few feet in front of me. She smiled.

"I just want to tell you that I don't think you should be worried about Ryan."

I looked up, surprised. She sounded so sure about it, as if she knew exactly what he was up to.

"What makes you say that?" I replied with amusement.

She sat herself down next to me and shrugged her shoulders.

"Think about it, Cecilia. He loves you. Ryan cares about you so much. He wouldn't give up on you that easily. At least give it a few days before you start really worrying about it. Maybe he just got sleepy and decided it best to ride out the storm."

I felt oddly reassured by her childish logic, but in all honesty, she was right. I needed to give Ryan more credit than that. I decided to wait a few more days before jumping to any big conclusions. Brittany and I made our way to the main room.

For now, everyone's main concern was turned toward the quickly approaching storm. Dr. Jenkins felt helpless for not being able to give us an accurate prediction of its strength, and my heart went out to him. I knew that this whole experience was starting to put a strain on him, and I knew that he deeply mourned his wife.

Michael and Henry had a story to tell. This was the second major storm to hit the city. The first one was two days ago. Both storms had approached the city quickly. They'd been able to see the dark clouds forming in the distance. They had a decent shelter during the first storm. But when the second one started today, they realized that they'd better head back to the shelter or it would become impossible to make it back.

"We searched for over half a day," Henry explained, slightly annoyed. "We would've stayed longer if the storms hadn't been a factor." He glanced at me.

I placed a smile on my face and tried to hide my annoyance. A half day? Did they not consider the fact that the

entire city had been completely demol-
ished? Surely, it would take longer to
search for someone?

My annoyance was replaced with
anger, and I decided now would be a
good time to change the subject.

Just as I was about to ask what
the plans were for the remainder of
the afternoon, I heard a large rumble
from outside. My heart froze, thinking
that we were about to endure another
earthquake.

"Thunder," Renee stated, looking
worriedly up toward the front of the
shelter.

Thunder? I had figured we were in
for a blizzard, not thunderstorms. It had
been so long since I'd heard thunder.

Then Dr. Jenkins's loud voice interrupted my thoughts. "Luckily, even if we were to be hit with some extreme or severe weather, we're technically living in a fortified basement. We should be safe as long as we stay in the lower floors of the shelter."

Although that eased some of my concerns, it didn't change the fact that Ryan wasn't underground. He was still out *there*, and for all we knew, he could be really hurt.

The anger that I had been feeling earlier returned, and I decided that maybe the nap I had been planning would serve me well after all. At least it would keep me from snapping at Henry and Michael. They had risked their butts for everyone. And they had brought back quite a lot of stuff.

Back in my room, I lay down in bed. I could still smell Ryan's scent on the sheets. I drew them closer and inhaled deeply, as if the bigger the breath I took, the better the chances were of him coming back in one piece. The dark room suddenly became soothing, and I found myself being lulled to sleep by the cool sheets and the low rumble of thunder in the distance.

Day 20

3:00 p.m.

I woke up to a large *boom*.

"Holy crap!" Jesska exclaimed, swerving quickly to the right.

A large tree had just fallen in the middle of the road. Jesska's eyes were wide, and she breathed heavily as we continued driving down the cluttered road.

Well, that's one way to wake someone up.

"What happened?" I asked, placing my hand on Jesska's thigh to calm her down.

She shook her head.

"I guess lightning hit that tree in the wrong spot. We intersected almost perfectly," she explained, regaining her composure.

The storm had hit the city full force. The wind blew in large gusts, and the trees that were still left standing looked as if they were hanging on by only their roots. What was strange was that instead of the snow we expected, rain was falling from the sky in thick sheets. It was completely unnatural for it to be this warm in Denver in the dead of winter. Every so often, large flashes of lightning cracked through the sky, followed by loud, ear-rattling thunder.

The scenery around us began to look familiar, and I knew we would be reaching the downtown area soon. I started to grow anxious, and I realized that the interrogation I was about to undergo with Cecilia could end badly.

I wanted Jesska to stay with us at the shelter. There was no way that she would ever be able to make it alone, no matter how much she thought she could. But as we drove, I began wondering if bringing them together so suddenly was a lousy idea.

"You're going to have to give me some sort of direction on how to get there eventually," Jesska commented, avoiding a huge steel beam in the road.

"Sure," I replied. "Just continue going straight on this road. There's an old cathedral that will be coming up soonish. When you see that, you're going to take a right."

Jesska nodded and tapped her fingers on the steering wheel.

"So what are you supposed to say, when you show up with me at the doorstep?"

She stared directly at the road. I took a deep breath, knowing that this conversation would come sooner or later.

"The truth," I stated. Now she turned to look at me, eyebrows raised.

"And that would be?"

I cleared my throat. "That I ran into you when I was searching for supplies.

You had a truck and knew of a place where we could get some significant essentials. I'll explain what happened with Jason, and how we had to stay at the warehouse for a couple of nights."

Her eyes dropped, and I realized that she must have thought that I was going to tell Cecilia about the kiss. I honestly hadn't even made up my mind about what I was going to do about that topic. I knew deep down that telling Cecilia would be the best answer, and yeah, she'd probably be pissed, but I'd rather her be mad at me than deal with the guilt of lying to her.

"I'll probably tell her about the kiss too," I noted quietly. Jesska tightened her grip on the steering wheel and continued driving.

"Why?" she asked.

"Because I can't keep anything from her," I explained. "She'll be mad at first. But really, Jesska, I'd rather her be mad at me than sense that I am keeping something like that from her."

Jesska nodded slightly. "That's fine. But understand something," she turned to look at me, "I don't regret it. And don't expect me to have a written apology if your girlfriend starts getting bitchy with me."

I sighed. I felt like this was some twisted apocalyptic soap opera.

"I'm not going to make you apologize, Jess," I said, glancing over at her. "And quite honestly, I don't regret it either. But that doesn't mean that I shouldn't be telling her what I've been up to."

We came to the mutual agreement that I would tell Cecilia what happened, and if anything were to break out between Jesska and Cecilia, I would put a stop to it.

After taking a right when we approached the now half-collapsed cathedral and driving a bit further on, I began to get anxious. I wondered if Michael and Henry had gone back to the shelter to let everyone know I was gone.

Jesska pulled up to the closest possible spot next to the shelter.

"Let's leave everything in here until we get done with our introductions," I suggested.

"Maybe we should bring some of it with us? That way it looks like you actually accomplished something during your absence."

I gave her credit for that suggestion, and we hauled out the supplies that I had packed for us. After six trips back and forth from the Hummer to the entrance of the shelter, we were ready to make our appearance.

Day 20

6:00 p.m.

After a long afternoon nap, I felt oddly refreshed. The troubling thoughts that had been pounding in my head before had stopped, and my anxiousness about Ryan wasn't as intense.

A delicious aroma seeped through my door, and my stomach growled. I realized I had skipped lunch. I was famished. I washed my face in the bathroom and tried to make my hair look somewhat acceptable. I was still fighting with my hair, even at the end of the world.

In the kitchen, Dr. Jenkins and Brittany were at the table playing Spit, and Renee stood cooking over the stove. It looked like a scene from the show *Seventh Heaven*—one big, happy family, immune to the troubles of the world, at least on the surface. It was good how close all of us had gotten. It gave us sort of a family feel; something that I think we all needed.

"Cecilia, you woke up!" Renee exclaimed, smiling. She walked over to me and embraced me in a hug. For some reason, this action reminded me of my mom. But instead of feeling sad about it, I felt almost comforted.

"Are you feeling better?" she asked quietly.

I pulled back from her and gave her a sincere smile.

"I am. Where are Michael and Henry?" I asked.

"They're showering or sleeping, I believe," Renee replied, returning to the stove.

"What are you making?" I asked curiously, my stomach growling.

Renee beamed. "Bean and corn soup! It doesn't sound good, but I guarantee that it's delicious. I promise. Michael and Henry were able to collect a lot of canned goods, so we have more dinner options now."

"Sounds good to me!" I declared.

Suddenly, a loud knock rang through the shelter. My heart lifted. Was it Ryan?

Renee looked up at me anxiously, and everyone in the room grew quiet.

"Do you want to go answer it, Cecilia?" Renee asked cautiously.

I decided I would. If it was Ryan, I would want to be alone with him as soon as I could. But the disappointment I would feel if it wasn't him was going to suck.

I walked slowly up the stairs to the main floor, where the knocking continued. At the top of the stairs, the rain pounded against the metal roof, almost drowning out the continuing thunder. I approached the large doors slowly, as if afraid of what may be behind them. In a way, I was.

I took a deep breath and struggled to pull the door open.

When I saw Ryan, his eyes lit up, and his dazzling smile made my heart melt as always. But as the door continued to open, my feelings quickly turned cold as I saw the companion he had decided to bring along with him.

Standing in front of me was a beautiful girl, the type you'd see in all of those teen movies. Her dark hair fell in perfect waves to her waist. Even in the big sweater and ripped jeans she was wearing, she could still pass as a model for *Vogue*. Who the hell was she?

I tilted my head and looked back and forth at them, wondering what in the world was going on. Ryan and I had *never* had a girl or guy come between us, and I never would've imagined it being a problem now, after all we had been through.

The three of us awkwardly looked at each other for a few moments before Ryan decided to try and break the ice.

"Babe!" he walked up to me and embraced me in a hug. Aside from being confused and sort of pissed off, feeling his body against mine again was reassuring, and I felt myself melt into him as I always did.

He placed his hand on the back of my head and kissed me on the cheek.

"I've missed you so much."

Instead of responding to him, I pulled away and opened the door as wide as I could against the wind to let him and his "friend" inside. They started bringing the supplies in, and I quickly realized that Ryan had been able to get *a lot* of supplies. A lot more than Henry and Michael, and a lot more than Renee or any of us were expecting.

"Where did you get all of this stuff, Ryan?" I asked curiously, ignoring the girl completely. She stood awkwardly off to the side of us with her arms crossed. Apparently, this was just as uncomfortable for her as it was for me.

He stepped back and pointed at the one "supply" he'd returned with that there was no way in hell he was going to keep.

Day 20

6:30 p.m.

"Cecilia, this is Jesska," Ryan muttered. "I ran into her when Michael and Henry and I split up. She was able to keep a functioning Hummer after the earthquake, and she took me to this Walmart distribution warehouse outside of the city."

Jesska looked up and stared at me. She offered a weak smile.

"Hey there," she mumbled.

I remained quiet and glared at Ryan. Something was definitely up. But it would have to wait.

"Ryan! Oh my God. Thank God you're safe!" Renee ran up to Ryan with her arms out and embraced him in a tight hug.

He blushed. "Sorry, Renee. I know I must've really scared you guys, but look at all of the stuff we scored!"

He pointed at the many boxes that were lined up against the wall, and Renee's jaw dropped.

"Good God! How did you manage to get all of it here?"

Just as she said that, she noticed Jesska. Renee glanced at me before walking over to where this new girl was standing.

"I feel so rude," she said, holding her hand out. "I'm Renee. I'm sure that you have something to do with all of this getting here. Let's go get you dried off and settled in, and then you can tell us all about it!"

After dinner, when I knew Jesska was off with Renee getting settled, I sat alone in our bedroom, thinking about everything that had happened over the course of the past several days. I couldn't believe that Jason had found Ryan. I knew that if Jesska hadn't been there with him, there was a good chance that he wouldn't have made it back here alive.

But something was off. I knew that there was more to the story than Ryan was telling me, and I wondered if he was going to tell me himself or if I was going to have to find it out on my own.

Just then, the door opened, and I looked up to see Ryan standing bashfully in the doorway.

"Can I join you?" he asked.

"Sure," I replied, scooting over.

He sat down next to me and placed his hand on my leg. I looked up at him and told myself that before I gave in to anything, I was going to get to the bottom of this.

"Baby, I've missed you so much," he murmured, putting his hand on my neck to pull me in for a kiss. I stiffened. Realizing my reluctance, he stopped and pulled back to look at me.

"Ryan, I want to know what happened," I stated hotly, staring into his eyes. "You have guilt written all over your face."

He looked down and sighed.

"Jesska's a pretty girl," he said, looking down at the ground.

I clenched my jaw. Had he slept with her?

He looked up at me and brushed back a piece of hair from my face.

"I kissed her," he said, keeping his hand on my face.

He said it so simply, I thought. As if it meant nothing. As if he hadn't just put two years of what we had on the line.

Before I could think about what I was doing, I reached out and slapped him across the face.

His eyes widened, and I gasped, almost as surprised as he was.

He began to say something, but then stopped and laughed.

My anger rose. Why in the world would he find this funny? After a few moments of watching him laugh, my anger began to recede, and the truth of what I had just done hit me. We weren't being filmed for a reality show. This was real life. He was the only person in the whole world who really *knew* me. I was the only person in the whole world who really *knew* him. Some girl who he met four days ago was not going to change that.

I began to giggle, and before we knew it, both of us were lying back on the bed laughing like we hadn't, in what seemed like months.

After he was breathing normally again, Ryan turned over and looked at me with a serious face.

"I wish your mom would've seen that slap." He paused and smiled. "She would have been so proud."

I giggled. My mom had always ranted on about how men should be whipped into shape.

"Why did you do it, Ryan?" I asked quietly, bringing the seriousness back to our talk.

He tilted his head back and sighed.

"Because I'm a guy, Cecilia," he said. "Jesska's a pretty girl. It was in the heat of the moment. She knows you're my girl. She knows how much I love you. And I am not about to mess up the beautiful thing that you and me have, baby," he whispered, pulling me close.

I felt his heart thump against his chest, and I knew that he was being sincere.

He kissed me and ran his lips against my ear.

"Can I ask you a favor?" he asked in a whisper.

I rolled my eyes. "What now?"

He leaned back and stretched his arms over his head.

"I want you to be nice to Jesska," he stated.

Hmm? I hadn't even thought about what I was going to do about the Jesska problem. Duh, I also didn't realize that she must be moving into the shelter with us.

"I don't know, Ryan," I said uncertainly. How would I know that I'd be able to trust them together?

He took my hands in his and smiled. "She's such a nice girl, Cecilia. If you forget about what happened between her and me, you two could grow to be good friends. She's a survivor. She's so tough on the outside, but I know she won't make it out there alone. I made it clear to her that what happened between us would never be repeated."

When I didn't reply, Ryan looked at me with pleading eyes. "Cecilia, come on. She's new here; she feels as if you hate her."

"Maybe I do," I replied bluntly. I didn't. But Ryan couldn't be let off the hook that easily.

After a few minutes of silence, I sighed and decided that I didn't really have much of a choice anyway. I planned on keeping my guard up, but I decided to handle this the mature way. I was growing up fast.

"Okay, Ryan, I'll talk to her." I said, giving in. "But if it happens again, I'm gone," I warned.

I didn't really know where I was supposed to go in the situation we were in, but I figured it was the most appropriate thing to say. I leaned over, kissed Ryan on the cheek, and we headed back out into the living room. It was time to meet her, my new friend.

Day 20

11:30 p.m.

I lay in bed and hit replay. Everything that had happened over the past few days was mind-blowing: First, I killed a guy. Yeah, he was a strung-out freak who was going to flatten me. But still. Second, I cheated on Cecilia. Kinda. Jesska was hard to resist. My mom would've smacked me if she'd heard my lame excuse—I'm just a dude.

In our old normal world, I would not be regarded as the most upstanding person. But luckily—poor choice of words—the world was anything but normal.

Cecilia had given in and made a proper introduction to Jesska. Though reluctant at first, Jesska began to open up, and I was hopeful that a friendship between the two would develop over time. Cecilia was a loyal person, and Jesska needed someone like that in her life. Jesska was a go-getter, and Cecilia needed to pick up a few pointers.

While I was dealing with drama, Michael and Henry unloaded the Hummer. Everyone in the shelter was beyond thankful for the supplies that we had brought back. Renee had made us a feast, the biggest meal we had eaten since the earthquake.

After dinner, we all met up in the living area and listened to an old Nirvana CD someone had left in the shelter and played cards. Jesska got to know everyone, and I'm pretty sure we all had her convinced that if you were going to be living in this mess of a world, the shelter was the place to be.

Later, Cecilia snored lightly beside me, and I smiled, happy to know that she was still mine. I was also glad to have met Jesska. The friendship that we had developed over the past few days, I had no doubt would last a lifetime.

I felt more at peace, and I had no trouble closing my eyes and drifting into a well-needed, relaxing sleep.

Day 21

6:00 a.m.

The next morning, I was immediately awakened by a crash. Cecilia also jerked awake, and even in the darkness of the room, I could tell she was panicked.

"What was that?" she asked uncertainly while blinking her eyes awake.

We could hear heavy footsteps above us on the main floor of the shelter. People?

"Guys, get up! Get out of your room," Renee commanded.

Holding Cecilia's hand, I opened the door to find Renee standing ashen-faced with Daniel on her hip and Brittany by her side.

"I don't know who it is," Renee cried fearfully.

Henry, Michael, Dr. J, and Jesska piled into the hallway as well.

"What should we do?" Renee asked, looking at Dr. J.

He chewed on his lip. I think he was getting tired of being the one who was supposed to have all of the answers.

"I'll go check it out," I offered. I'd been through so much already that fear didn't play a huge a role in my life. Nobody argued. The footsteps continued on the main floor.

I walked slowly to the large metal doors that led to the main floor of the building. I took a deep breath and figured that whatever it was, I'd been through worse.

I shoved open the doors at the top of the staircase and walked onto the main floor.

I gasped. The doors to the ground-floor shelter had been pushed open. Outside, I could see the flash of red lights.

"Young man!" a voice echoed. I looked over to the left and saw an African American man in an army uniform standing there.

I was taken by such surprise that I couldn't find any words to say back to him.

The man walked up to me and placed his hands on my shoulders.

"Young man, are you okay? My name is Sergeant Myles. I'm escorting a Red Cross emergency team through the area. Is there anyone else here with you?"

I nodded, still speechless. There was help? There were more people alive? Thousands of thoughts and questions ran through my head.

"Yes, sir. Wait here! Oh my gosh. There are nine of us. I think. Yes, nine. Wait right here. I'll be back."

Before he could respond, I ran to get everyone from downstairs. At first, they refused to believe me, but once brought upstairs, their doubts were confirmed wrong.

Aside from Sergeant Myles, there were six other rescue workers. Unlike him, they were dressed in blue jeans and white T-shirts.

"Do you know what's supposed to happen next?" Jesska asked.

I think we all wondered the same thing.

"We'll be able to explain that to you better once we get you guys to the camps."

Camps? That kind of label gave it a sort of World War II creepiness.

I think all of our faces registered the same reaction, because one of the rescue workers chuckled.

"Don't worry. It's a camp for survivors. We have food and water, and there are other people already there.

We also have a little bit more information about how this event has impacted the rest of the world. Everything will be explained there."

My spirits lifted. There were more survivors! There was still some form of government! I felt all the hope that I had lost over the past month return. For the first time, I truly felt like things would be okay.

After some hurried packing, the rescue workers and our small crew were able to load the majority our supplies and other usable items from the shelter into trucks that looked built to handle the awful road conditions. They assured us that all of the stuff we had collected would be ours to keep.

I got Jesska alone for a few moments and embraced her in a hug. "Aren't you so glad that you came here?" I said, grinning. "They may not have found you in that piece-of-crap house you were so fond of before."

She playfully hit my shoulder. "Shut up, Ryan."

"Seriously, are you going to be okay? Are you okay with all this?" I hinted.

"You mean the camp or do you mean with your girl? Because I don't have a problem with either. Look, you need to be needed, and I don't need you. She does," Jesska replied.

She walked off, and I got to admire her all over again. She was one hot chick who was going to be okay wherever she ended up.

They would be taking us to the closest survivors camp, which was in Santa Fe, New Mexico. Sergeant Myles explained that there were many, many teams of rescue workers, but communication systems were spotty, the weather was challenging, and the infrastructure was toast. We were lucky that they found us at all.

It was decided that Henry, Michael, Daniel, Renee, and Brittany would ride in one truck, while Dr. J, Cecilia, Jesska, and I would ride in the other. We were promised that they wouldn't split us up, and I had no problem placing my trust in them.

Once we piled into the trucks, I looked out of the back and stared at the shelter. I realized that we would probably never be returning. Although our stay here was brief, I knew that the past few weeks had given me enough life-lessons and memories to last forever.

I looked at Cecilia and Jesska and smiled. They both returned full-blown grins. Dr. J heaved a huge sigh and closed his eyes. Sergeant Myles sat with us. As we started driving away, he began talking to us about other catastrophes that had happened around the world, and how they thought the different events were connected. I really wanted to know who he meant by *they*, but I didn't ask. That was a question for another time.

I placed my hand on Cecilia's, and she turned and offered me the million-dollar smile that I had fallen in love with two years ago. I saw the shelter growing smaller and smaller behind us. As the wind whipped up a little, I realized that we would probably never come back to Denver. As we continued driving, we left behind many of the doubts, worries, and concerns that had been weighing us down for almost three weeks.

After the devastation, the shelter was our new normal. And now we were leaving it behind and were heading into the unknown. But instead of seeing that as a bad thing, I was hopeful for a better future—certainly we would not have survived at the shelter for much longer. Cecilia squeezed my hand, and we both faced forward. Together, we were ready to face the new opportunities and challenges that were ahead of us: our new normal.

About the Author

Sara Michelle

As a high school student, I never thought that I could pursue my creative interests. But with the support of my family, I auditioned to attend an arts magnet program in south-central Texas. I'm so excited to be going to a school that lets me explore my right brain and harnesses my imagination.

Speaking of interests ... those would involve: singing, songwriting, dancing, reading, going out with friends, spending money, and—writing. I love this time in my life and plan to live it up while doing what I used to believe was impossible, writing and publishing books. One day I'd love to get my PhD in psychology—and in a parallel universe, I'd love to be an actor. My favorite food is ice cream; I could honestly live off of it 24/7. My friends mean the world to me, and I'd be absolutely nowhere without my large, crazy family. I can't wait to see what life has to offer, and I plan on enjoying every minute of it!